Dear Parent:
Your child's love of reading sta

Every child learns to read in a different way and at his or her own speed. Some go back and forth between reading levels and read favorite books again and again. Others read through each level in order. You can help your young reader improve and become more confident by encouraging his or her own interests and abilities. From books your child reads with you to the first books he or she reads alone, there are I Can Read Books for every stage of reading:

SHARED READING
Basic language, word repetition, and whimsical illustrations, ideal for sharing with your emergent reader

BEGINNING READING
Short sentences, familiar words, and simple concepts for children eager to read on their own

READING WITH HELP
Engaging stories, longer sentences, and language play for developing readers

READING ALONE
Complex plots, challenging vocabulary, and high-interest topics for the independent reader

I Can Read Books have introduced children to the joy of reading since 1957. Featuring award-winning authors and illustrators and a fabulous cast of beloved characters, I Can Read Books set the standard for beginning readers.

A lifetime of discovery begins with the magical words **"I Can Read!"**

Visit www.icanread.com for information
on enriching your child's reading experience.

I Can Read® and I Can Read Book® are trademarks of HarperCollins Publishers.

Baby Shark's Big Show!: Meet the Shark Family and Friends

Printed in the United States of America.

For information address HarperCollins Children's Books, a division of
HarperCollins Publishers, 195 Broadway, New York, NY 10007.
www.icanread.com

ISBN 978-0-06-315885-6

Typography by Elaine Lopez-Levine
22 23 24 25 LSCC 10 9 8 7 6 5 4 3 2

First Edition

BABY SHARK'S BIG SHOW!™

pinkfong

Meet the Shark Family and Friends

Adapted by Alexandra West

HARPER
An Imprint of HarperCollins*Publishers*

nickelodeon

Meet Baby Shark.
Baby Shark is sweet,
bubbly, and fearless!

He’s a happy shark who loves
to show off his shark toothy smile!

Most of his fish friends call
Baby Shark by his first name.
Baby!
Baby likes to take on big adventures.
He always has his friends and family
there to help him.

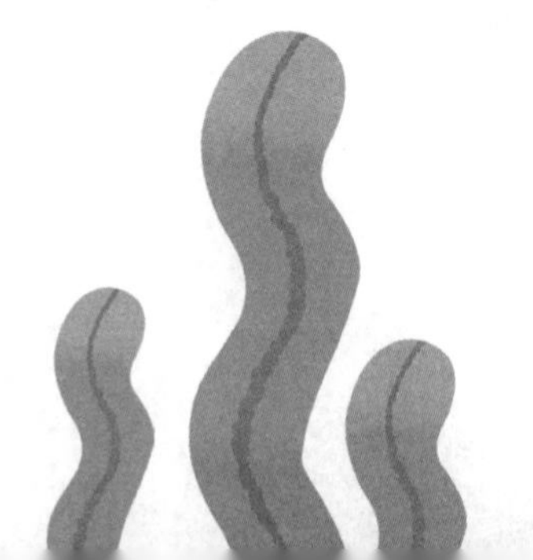

This is Mommy Shark.

Whether she is playing a board game or working, she is a winner!

Mommy Shark works for the mayor.
Some say she is fiercely fun.
In Baby's eyes, she's the
coolest fishy in the sea.

Then there is Daddy Shark.
As a shark tooth dentist,
he loves to make everyone smile!
He can't help his loud,
goofy nature.
Sometimes he even flosses
his own teeth when he's nervous!

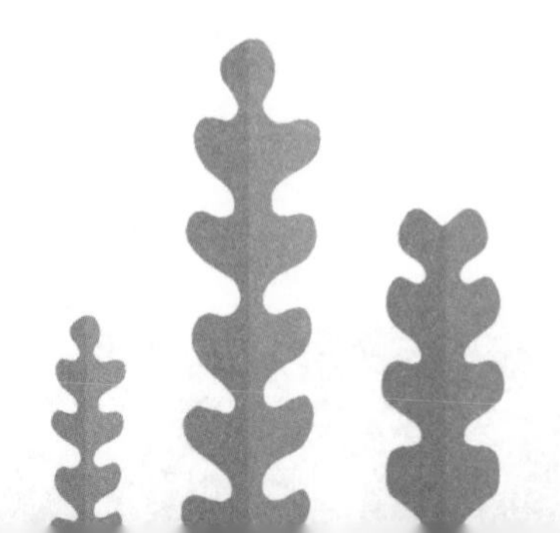

Meet Grandma Shark.
Grandma is all good vibes
and bubbleberry pies.

She loves meditating so she can be gentle and calming.

This is Grandpa Shark.

Grandpa has charm up to the gills.

He always has a whale of a tale to tell!

Every fishy loves listening to his

stories about the old days.

Even if some of his stories

sound super silly and made-up!

Not only does Baby love his family,

but he also loves his friends.

No matter how choppy the water gets,

they can always make him smile.

Baby can always find his friends
at the Wreck.
That's the playground.

This is William.

A careful fish, William is always

there to help his best friend.

This fish isn't afraid to get

things done.

Where there's a William,

there's a way!

William lives next door to Baby. He is Baby's best bud in the whole wide water.

With a friend like William,
life is always an adventure!

Vola is one cute and cool octopus!
Octopuses are great at blending in,
but Vola would rather stand out.
With eight legs and eight brains,
Vola can do anything.
Like ride on her skatefish board!

This is Hank.

Hank is a whale fish.

He even has a tiny blowhole!

And check out those rosy cheeks.

His sweet nature means that

Hank is pure goodness.

He has a pet rock named Rocky!

Then there is Goldie.

Goldie is a goldfish with a sparkling personality.

Goldie loves all things glitzy
and glamorous.
She loves to put on a show!

And then there is Chucks.
He is one super chill dude.
Chucks is great at going
with the flow.
While his ideas may seem silly,
they are usually really good!

Baby and his friends love adventure. But most of all, they are just happy to spend time together.

These fishy friends sing
and dance all day.
They shake their cares away.
Come on, shake your tail fin!

With friends and family like these,
there's nothing Baby can't doo-doo-doo!